12/2021

DREAMWORKS
Rhyme Time TOWN
MS. MACDONALD HAS A FARM

Adapted by May Nakamura

Ready-to-Read

Simon Spotlight
New York   London   Toronto   Sydney   New Delhi

SIMON SPOTLIGHT

An imprint of Simon & Schuster Children's Publishing Division
1230 Avenue of the Americas, New York, New York 10020
This Simon Spotlight edition August 2021
DreamWorks Rhyme Time Town © 2021 DreamWorks Animation LLC.
All Rights Reserved.

SIMON SPOTLIGHT, READY-TO-READ, and colophon are registered trademarks of
Simon & Schuster, Inc. For information about special discounts for bulk purchases,
please contact Simon & Schuster Special Sales at 1-866-506-1949
or business@simonandschuster.com.
Manufactured in the United States of America 0721 LAK
10 9 8 7 6 5 4 3 2 1
ISBN 978-1-5344-9399-5 (hc)
ISBN 978-1-5344-9398-8 (pbk)
ISBN 978-1-5344-9400-8 (eBook)

Daisy and Cole are farmers for a day!

They will take care of
the farm animals.

"You will need to close the gate," Ms. MacDonald says.

"Then, let the animals out of the barn."

"Easy-peasy!" Cole says.

Ms. MacDonald
and Lucy Goosey
leave for the market.

Humpty Dumpty
and Mary Mary walk by.

They want
to be farmers too.

Humpty opens
the barn door.

Uh-oh!
They forgot to
close the gate!

All the animals run away!

Cole has an idea.

They put down
lines of corn and hay.

The ducks come to eat.

But the farm animals
do not come back
to the barn.

Humpty has an idea.
They drive tractors
through the town.

The farmers try to
round up the animals,
but they all run away.

"Maybe we can sing
like farmers,"
Daisy says.

"Ms. MacDonald
has a farm, *E-I-E-I-O!*"
they sing.

"And on that farm
she has some cows,
E-I-E-I-O!"

"With a *moo-moo* here and a *moo-moo* there, here a *moo*, there a *moo*, everywhere a *moo-moo*!"

"Ms. MacDonald
has a farm, *E-I-E-I-O*!"
they continue.

"And on that farm
she has some sheep,
E-I-E-I-O!"

The farmers sing
for all the animals.

The animals like
the song.
They come back
to the farm!

Then Ms. MacDonald

returns to the farm.

"What happy animals!"
Ms. MacDonald says.
"Thank you,
little farmers!"

Everyone sings together.
"Ms. MacDonald
has a farm, *E-I-E-I-O*!"